Thoughtful Thinking

Haikus for Children

Daksha Patel

Illustrated By Izzy Bean

Grosvenor House
Publishing Limited

This book is published by
Grosvenor House Publishing Ltd
Link House
140 The Broadway, Tolworth, Surrey, KT6 7HT.
www.grosvenorhousepublishing.co.uk

A CIP record for this book
is available from the British Library

ISBN 978-1-80381-311-0
eBook ISBN 978-1-80381-312-7

Dedication

I dedicate this book to my family
and to my role model
Swami Vivekananda

This Book belongs to:

CONTENTS

ABOUT THE AUTHOR

Daksha Patel is of Indian origin. She was born in October 1975. She has a BA Honours Degree in English with History. She also has a Post Graduate Certificate in Primary Education that includes Qualified Teacher Status from Brunel University.

Daksha is fluent in Gujarati and holds a purple belt in the martial art of Karate.

Daksha Patel's motto in life is that 'if at first you don't succeed in your aims and objectives then you should try, try and try again'. Education is for character building and enables us to shine like stars when we succeed at it.

QUESTION:

What is a Haiku?

ANSWER:

Haikus are poems from Japan -they have 3 lines and 17 syllables in total. The lines are in the order of 5,7,5 syllables.

You can count the syllables on your fingers.

HAIKU: THE CARTOON CHARACTER

The top cartoon cat,
He has a spotty bow tie.
And wears a nice suit.

HAIKU: THE CARTOON CHARACTER

Comprehension

1) What clothes is the cat wearing?

2) Do you like cats?

3) Do you watch cartoons?

4) What are some famous cartoon cats on TV?

5) How many lives does a cat have?

HAIKU: POTATOES

Crispy potatoes,
They fry slowly in the pan,
Sizzling in oil.

HAIKU: POTATOES

Comprehension

1) In the poem, how are the potatoes being cooked?

2) Does the oil in the pan make the potatoes crispy?

3) What is the sound word in the poem?

4) What are chips made of?

5) Have you ever used a frying pan?

HAIKU: COOKIES

Chocolate chip cookies,
They crumble inside your mouth.
The cookies taste sweet.

HAIKU: COOKIES

Comprehension

1) What type of cookies is this about?

2) How do the cookies feel in the mouth?

3) Are the cookies sweet in taste?

4) Is the taste of the cookies more important then how they look?

5) Do you like eating cookies?

HAIKU: ROSES

Ruby red roses,
Their petals feel velvety.
Their smell is intense.

HAIKU: ROSES

Comprehension

1) What colour are the roses in the poem?

2) How do the petals of the roses feel in the poem?

3) Is the smell of the roses strong?

4) Do you like the smell of roses?

5) Have you ever been given roses?

HAIKU: BEEHIVE

Sweet scent of honey
Roaming the fresh morning air.
The bees hard at work.

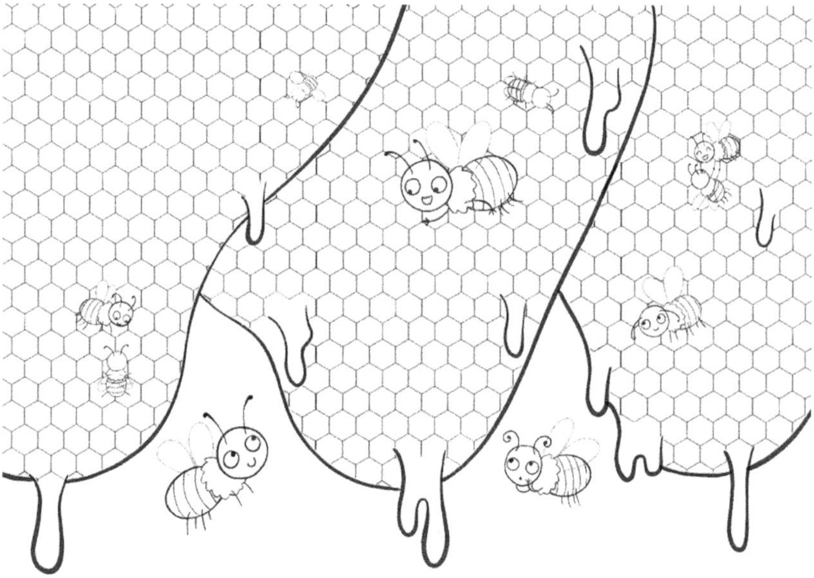

HAIKU: BEEHIVE

Comprehension

1) Does the honey smell sweet?

2) Why are the bees hard at work?

3) Are bees dangerous to humans?

4) Have you ever been stung by a bee?

5) Have you ever tasted honey made by bees?

HAIKU: APPLE ORCHARD

It is the ripe smell
Of apples that lingers in
The cold morning air.

HAIKU: APPLE ORCHARD

Comprehension

1) What is an orchard?

2) Do you eat apples?

3) Are all apples green?

4) How do you know when an apple is rotten?

5) How many different ways is there to eat an apple?

HAIKU: PIZZA POEM

A round pizza base,
With tasty toppings on it.
Cheese stretching like lace.

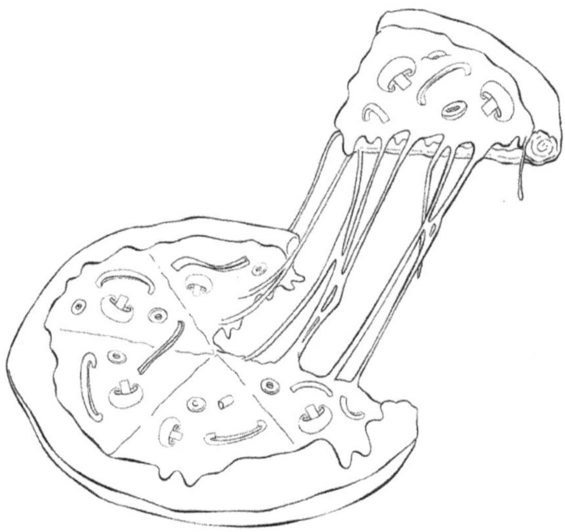

HAIKU: PIZZA POEM

Comprehension

1) What shape is the pizza base?

2) What is stretching like lace?

3) What sort of toppings can you get on a pizza?

4) Have you ever tasted a pizza?

5) Have you ever made your own pizza?

HAIKU: STRAWBERRY PICKING POEM

Seeds on the outside,
With red, bumpy flesh to eat.
Hands picking quickly.

HAIKU: STRAWBERRY PICKING POEM

Comprehension

1) Where are the seeds of the strawberries?

2) Have you ever been to a strawberry farm?

3) Have you ever eaten strawberries?

4) Why are the strawberries being picked quickly?

5) Are strawberries healthy for you?

HAIKU: NOODLES

Noodles in a bowl,
The chop sticks are on the side.
The noodles are long.

HAIKU: NOODLES

Comprehension

1) Are the noodles in the poem in a bowl or plate?

2) What are chop sticks for?

3) Have you ever used chop sticks to eat food with?

4) Are the noodles long or short?

5) Have you ever eaten noodles?

HAIKU: AT THE SWIMMING POOL

Down the water slide,
And straight into the blue pool,
Swimming in water.

HAIKU: AT THE SWIMMING POOL

Comprehension

1) What colour is the water in the swimming pool?

2) Can you swim?

3) Is the skill of swimming important?

4) Have you ever been down a water slide?

5) Can you float in water?

ANSWERS TO THE

Comprehensions

1) Haiku: The Cartoon Character

    1. A spotty bow tie and a nice suit.
    2. Yes or No.
    3. Yes or No.
    4. Tom from Tom & Jerry, Garfield, Top Cat, etc.
    5. One.

2) Haiku: Potatoes

    1. They are frying in oil.
    2. Yes.
    3. Sizzling.
    4. Potatoes.
    5. Yes or No.

3) Haiku: Cookies

1. Chocolate chip cookies.
2. Crumbly.
3. Yes.
4. Yes.
5. Yes or No.

4) Haiku: Roses

1. Red.
2. Velvety.
3. Yes.
4. Yes or No.
5. Yes or No.

5) Haiku: Beehive

1. Yes.
2. They are busy collecting nectar to make honey in the beehive. Also, they are busy pollinating flowers.

3. Yes.
4. Yes or No.
5. Yes or No.

6) Haiku: Apple Orchard

1. An apple farm.
2. Yes or No.
3. No.
4. It looks bad and it smells.
5. You can eat it raw, cook it, boil it, fry it, steam it, grill it, air fry it and juice it.

7) Haiku: Pizza Poem

1. Round.
2. Cheese.
3. Quorn, meat, fish, vegetables, fruit, cheeses and herbs.
4. Yes or No.
5. Yes or No.

8) Haiku: Strawberry Picking Poem

1. On the outside of each berry.
2. Yes or No.
3. Yes or No.
4. So they don't spoil.
5. Yes.

9) Haiku: Noodles

1. In a bowl.
2. Eating food with.
3. Yes or No.
4. Long.
5. Yes or No.

10) Haiku: At the Swimming Pool

1. Blue.
2. Yes or No.
3. Yes.
4. Yes or No.
5. Yes or No.

BIBLIOGRAPHY

Books read:

- First Poems by Robert Fisher, Nash Pollock Publishing, 2000.
- Poems for Thinking by Robert Fisher, Nash Pollock Publishing, 1997.

Art Work:

- Black & white pictures to colour in by Izzy Bean (The Illustrator).

Websites used for coloured pictures:

http://stock.adobe.com
- Picture of child eating with chop sticks (on the front cover).
- Picture of roses (on the back cover).

NOTES

NOTES

NOTES

Lightning Source UK Ltd.
Milton Keynes UK
UKHW011030031222
413263UK00001B/63

9 781803 813110